To my dear friend
Dr. Jim Wagner
—L.R.R.

To Henry
—B.H.

BEAR'S BIG BREAKFAST

By
Lynn Rowe Reed

Illustrated by
Brett Helquist

SCHOLASTIC INC.

I'm starved.
I feel like breakfast.

Hello there, **Bunny**.
I am famished.

What are you in the mood for?

I can't remember.
I know it starts with
the letter

B....

Surely not a bunny.
I am too skinny
to taste good.

I'll help you find
a yummier breakfast.

Good morning, **Bumblebee**.
Do you taste good?

Of course! I am delicious. But
let me give you a kiss before you
eat me up.

I've changed my mind.

Then I will help you find breakfast.

Hola, **Boa!**
We come in peace.
I am looking for something
to eat, like maybe a
b-b-b-b-b—
I forget.

Here, try this bark.

Bark is not tasty!

Then we will
find you something
with more flavor.

I am hungrier than ever. I am so hungry I could eat a **bat**!

Wait! I am too bony for bears!
I will help you find a better breakfast.

Howdy, **Bluebird**!
Will you be my breakfast?

I would, Bear, but who will
take care of my beautiful babies?
I'll help you look for breakfast!

I am *so-o-o-o-o* sleepy.

I think . . . I need . . .

a nap.

ISBN 978-1-338-29052-3

Text copyright © 2016 by Lynn Rowe Reed. Illustrations copyright © 2016 by Brett Helquist. All rights reserved. Published by Scholastic Inc., 557 Broadway, New York, NY 10012, by arrangement with Balzer + Bray, an imprint of HarperCollins Children's Books, a division of HarperCollins Publishers. SCHOLASTIC and associated logos are trademarks and/or registered trademarks of Scholastic Inc.

12 11 10 9 8 7 6 5 4 3 2 1   18 19 20 21 22 23

Printed in the U.S.A.   40

First Scholastic printing, March 2018

The artist used acrylic and oil paints to create the illustrations for this book.
Typography by Dana Fritts